Happy tails to you!
"Mama" Marla
and

Sugar

Can Sugar come out to play?

Can **Sugar** come out to play?

by Marla Stahl

Once there was a little black dog who had come to live in her new home with her new mama.

Her mama named her Sugar because she was so very sweet.

Sugar was a rescue dog. Rescue dogs are very lucky dogs, because they get to be adopted by families who promise to love them and take good care of them forever.

When Sugar met her new mama and went to her new home, she was a little scared at first, but she soon found out that this mama would only give her lots and lots of love. And food! Delicious food! When Sugar first walked into her new home, she couldn't believe her eyes! There were comfy sofas and beds to sleep on, balls to play with (her favorite!) and the best part of all was a huge and beautiful back yard! Sugar's tail began to wag and wag. Her favorite thing (besides eating, of course!) was to run, run, run like the wind in the grass and around the trees.

"WOW, this is all mine!" Sugar said. "I am a very lucky dog!" Sugar was so happy!

Mama said, "Oh, Sugar, you are the perfect little dog! I will always love you, no matter what!" Mama was so happy!

One day Sugar and Mama were outside in the yard. Mama's neighbor came over to the fence to tell Mama a story. Sugar wandered around the yard.

She started sniffing and sniffing in the grass. She heard something. Uh-oh! What was it?

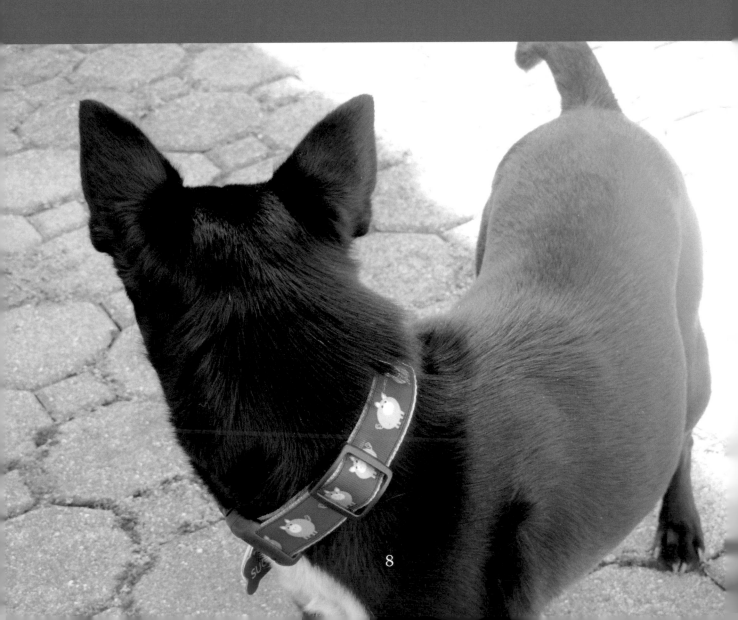

Suddenly, Mama heard all the birds making lots of noise, and sounding very, very angry. Mama ran to see what was the matter, and saw Sugar chasing a little bird.

"NO!!!!," cried Mama. "You can't scare the birds! They are our friends!"

Sugar felt sad, because Mama was upset. Mama explained, "The birds live in our yard, too. They love to sing, and they sing pretty songs to us every morning and every night. Their songs make me happy. Our beautiful trees in our yard make them happy. We have to share." Sugar wasn't too sure why they had to share, since it was her yard! But she didn't want Mama to be upset.

"OK, I'll try to remember," said Sugar.

Mama said, "It's OK, Sugar. You are still learning. You are the perfect little dog. I will always love you, no matter what!" Mama and Sugar had a hug, and they both felt better. She knew that her mama would only give her lots of love, no matter what—even if she was naughty. She felt so lucky!

The next day, Sugar and Mama were out in the yard, and Sugar was so happy that she ran in big circles around the trees, and around her mama.

'Wheeeeee!" She ran around and around! Sugar was fast, and it looked so funny! Mama laughed and laughed! After all that running, they went inside and Mama gave Sugar a snack.

"I am a very lucky dog!," she said. Sugar was so happy!

"Oh, Sugar, you are the perfect little dog!," said Mama. "You make me laugh! I will always love you, no matter what!" Mama was so happy!

That night, a chipmunk ran into Mama and Sugar's yard. Sugar tried to chase it, but Mama knew that might happen, so she had taken Sugar out on a leash. Mama held on tight. The chipmunk scurried away.

"Remember, Sugar, we have to share our yard with the other animals," said Mama.

"Chipmunks, TOO?," asked Sugar.

"Yes, chipmunks, too," replied Mama.

Then a froggie hopped by, and guess what Sugar wanted to do? That's right! She wanted to chase it! But Mama said no.

"Froggies, TOO?," asked Sugar. She was not happy about this.

"Yes, Sugar, froggies, too. We need to share our yard with all the animals. But we have our own special place inside our house. You have the whole house to run and play in—you only have to share it with me!"

Mama smiled.

Sugar felt a little grumpy. She wanted to chase the birds, bunnies, chipmunks, frogs, and even the butterflies! Sugar let out a big sigh.

But she had to admit that she had so much fun running in circles around the trees and Mama, and making Mama laugh, that she still loved her yard—even if sometimes she had to share it! And she loved playing and snuggling with Mama in the house. And she loved her food! She felt like the luckiest dog in the universe!

Sugar and Mama were happier and happier together with every new day. Every day, Mama said, "Oh, Sugar, you are the perfect little dog! I will always love you, no matter what!" Mama was so happy! Sugar was so happy!

One day something amazing happened. After breakfast, Sugar went to take a nap in one of her favorite sleepy spots. Mama was in the kitchen and heard a tapping on the glass patio door. She turned around and there, peeking in the door, was... a frog!

"Can Sugar come out to play?," he asked.

Mama was surprised. She said, "Sugar is taking a nap, but maybe later she can come out to play with you." Mama wondered if that would be a good idea. She was afraid Sugar would chase the frog and scare him, but Froggie didn't seem to mind.

"Thank you!," said Froggie. "See you later!" Before he scampered off, he peeked through the dining room window to see if he could wave hi to Sugar...

... but she was fast asleep.

That evening, after dinner, Sugar took another nap. She was very sleepy after all the running in circles she had done that day! While Sugar slept, Mama was looking out the window at the sunset, and a bunny came running up and looked right at her. Then Mama noticed another bunny sitting right under the open dining room window, and he was looking at her, too.

"Excuse me, but can Sugar come out to play before it gets dark?"

Mama was surprised, but she was happy that the animals wanted to play with her sweet little girl.

"Sugar is taking a nap after a very busy day. Maybe she can come out tomorrow," said Mama. "Thank you for asking!"

The very next morning when Mama opened the curtains, there was a bird looking right back at her, sitting at the bottom of the stairs.

"Is Sugar ready to come out and play?," asked the bird. Oh, my! Mama was so surprised.

"Sugar can come outside after breakfast," replied Mama. But the bird decided to come back later and flew away.

Mama wasn't sure why the other animals were no longer afraid of Sugar, but she thought that maybe it was because Sugar had a much better attitude about sharing the yard with them, and they knew it. Yay for Sugar!

Every morning after that, the birds, bunnies, chipmunks, and frogs waited for Sugar's mommy to open the curtains and see them all waiting outside for Sugar to go out and play. After she had her breakfast, Sugar asked Mama if she could go out to play with her new little friends. And so she did! She was so happy to see them!

They were so happy to see her! They romped and played and ran all over the yard together, sometimes stopping to munch on a leaf or flower. Even the butterflies joined in the fun!

Mama was so happy. She said, "Oh, Sugar, you are the perfect little dog! I will always love you, no matter what!" Sugar was so happy, too. Sugar loved her Mama, her house, her food, her yard, and even her new little animal friends! She had learned that when you share, you make others happy, you make new friends to have fun with, and it all feels great! Yay for Sugar, the perfect little dog, who will always be loved, no matter what!

The real "Mama" and Sugar live in Maryland, where Mama has raised three terrific little black rescue dogs and two wonderful children, and has two special "grand-doggies." In her spare time, she is a drummer in a church band and a tour guide for a major league baseball team. In addition to chasing bunnies and birds, Sugar's favorite pastimes are eating, napping, taking walks, running in circles around Mama and the trees, and snuggling with Mama.

CPSIA information can be obtained at www.ICGtesting.com
Printed in the USA
BVIW12n0931120416
443875BV00003B/4